Raymond Briggs'
The
Snowman™

Ladybird

It was morning, and as soon as he opened his eyes and saw the bright, white light coming through the window,

THE SNOWMAN the animated film is available on Polygram video
THE SNOWMAN is a TVC London production.
director DIANNE JACKSON supervising director JIMMY MURAKAMI
producer JOHN COATES executive producer IAIN HARVEY
music and lyrics by HOWARD BLAKE

Published by Ladybird Books Ltd.
A subsidiary of the Penguin Group
A Pearson Company

LADYBIRD and the associated pictorial device are trademarks of
Ladybird Books Ltd. Loughborough Leicestershire U.K.

James knew it would be a magical day…

It was **SNOWING!**

He'd never **got** dressed so **qui** — Hardly time **fo**r breakfast!

At *last* he was outside, **making** giant footprints in the snow **an**d throwing snowballs.

He began to roll a huge snowball and suddenly had an idea. The *best* thing to do would be to make a... SNOWMAN.

A big, big body.

A quick lunch—no time to stop!

A big round head.

Coal eyes, a tangerine nose, a hat and scarf, and last of all... James drew a mouth with his finger.

His snowman was finished.

His snowman was *smiling*!

Soon it was time for bed...

but it's hard to sleep when you're thinking of a snowman outside, all alone.

James got up and went out into the night. The day had been special...

but *this* was magical.
The snowman waved,
raised his hat,

and walked
toward
the house.

James took the snowman's hand,
and they went inside.

Ordinary snowmen *never* go inside a house, but *this* snowman wanted to see everything.

The fridge was best—it was cold, just the way snowmen like it!

Upstairs, Mom and Dad were fast asleep.

The snowman tried everything —including Mom's perfume, which nearly made him… sneeze!

The snowman
danced to a
music
box
and played
with James's
toys.

Mom and Dad didn't wake up.

Back outside they rode through the fields and forests on Dad's motorcycle...

But the snowman needed to be cold, and the motorcycle made his legs very hot.

So James took the snowman to the big freezer and soon ...the snowman's legs were fixed.

Then suddenly the snowman stopped smiling and listened.

What could he hear? Was he remembering something?

Then he began to run across the snow. James ran with him. He caught the snowman's hand and… all at once…

they were walking in the air…

looking far below…
holding very tight…

and flying
across the
world.

When at last they landed, the snowman led James through dark, dark woods…

until they came upon the most amazing sight that James could ever have imagined.

All the snowmen and snow-women in the world had come for a party!

And there was Santa Claus!
He gave James a present—
and a hug.

Then they all ate
and drank and
danced and
danced…

and danced…

until it was time to go home.

They
flew
back the
same way they
had come…

and soon they landed safely in
James's yard.

The snowman stood where
James had first made him...

but then James
ran back, gave
him one last
hug…

and
whispered,
"Thank you."

Next morning the sun was shining. James leaped out of bed, rushed down the stairs, and ran outside to see his very special snowman.

He couldn't believe his eyes as he walked toward a heap of melted snow, and a hat, a scarf, a tangerine, and some pieces of coal.

Had he been dreaming?

James felt in his bathrobe pocket and pulled out a snowman scarf— his present, given to him by Santa Claus, far away on one magical night.